Merlin
and the
Hidden Grove

A Magical Adventure

By Sandi Sanders

Dedication:

For all the children who see magic in everyday things and for every child's furry friend who delivers that magic and keeps their secrets safe. For curious young minds, dreamers and seekers with kind and caring hearts, may you always find wonder waiting just beyond the windowsill and carry joy and thrill with you on every adventure.

Table of Contents

Chapter 1

The Windowsill

Merlin was no ordinary cat. His coat shimmered like burnished copper, a ruddy Somali cat with a plume-like tail that curled elegantly over the windowsill.

On sunny mornings he claimed that sill as his throne, watching the garden sway below in a sea of colors. Birds flicked across the sky, bees tumbled lazily between flowers, and a little girl named Lila often perched outside on the fence with her green sketchbook pressed close.

Lila was eight years old and was quite an artist. She drew everything. She had once tried to sketch Merlin asleep, though he'd cracked one eye open and twitched his tail, making her giggle.

She didn't know that Merlin watched her, too. Not just the way humans notice, but with the keen awareness of a creature born with secrets.

That day, Merlin's eyes caught something unusual in the breeze. A glimmer that did not belong to pollen or sunshine. He leaned forward, whiskers twitching. Lila saw it too, a faint silver speck twisting in the air.

FUN FACT:

Somali cats, like Merlin, are curious and playful. They often perch in high spots, watching carefully. Just like Merlin on the windowsill.

Chapter 2
The Silver Leaf

The speck drifted closer until it landed in the grass. A single leaf with veins that gleamed like molten silver.

Lila gasped and crouched to draw it, her pencil scratching furiously. Merlin leapt from the sill to investigate. He sniffed the leaf and pawed it. It shimmered in response, as if it were alive. It understood.

"What do you think it is, Merlin?" Lila whispered.

He flicked his tail and looked at her with those bright green eyes that seemed to say "follow it".

And as though obeying him, the silver leaf rose gently into the air and drifted toward the old oak tree at the far end of the garden.

Lila tucked her sketchbook under her arm and, with much enthusiasm, followed.

Merlin trotted beside her, his tail held high and alert.

FUN FACT:

Leaves have veins that carry water and nutrients, just like veins in our bodies carry blood and oxygen. Some plants have very unique markings and colors that make them very special, just like Somali cats are unique and special.

Chapter 3
Know All Oliver

The oak tree was older than the house itself. Its bark bore carved initials from decades past, and its branches arched like wise arms.

On one of those branches perched a magnificent owl, snowy feathers brushed with silver. Mister Oliver.

"Well, well," boomed the owl, adjusting tiny round

spectacles on his beak. "You found the first sign, young seekers."

Lila froze in wonder, taking a moment to adjust her thoughts, before excitedly exclaiming in near disbelief, "The owl talks!"

"Of course I do," Oliver said with a chuckle. "And Merlin

already knows me, don't you, lad?" Merlin meowed softly. Indeed, they had met.

Throughout Merlin's lineage. Somali cats had long guarded magical, historical secrets in partnership with Mr. Oliver, the wise old, trusted owl.

"The leaf is your invitation," said the owl. "A journey awaits you, but only if you are so brave as to begin such an unknown journey."

Lila clutched her sketchbook tighter. Her heart pounded, but she nodded and then excitedly exclaimed, "Let's go!" And Merlin showed no hesitation.

FUN FACT:

Owls can turn their heads almost all the way around to see in many directions. They are symbols of wisdom in stories and in real life.

Chapter 4

Tiko's River

The silver leaf floated onward with a gentle breeze, leading them past the oak, and across fields, until they reached a rippling river. It's surface reflected more than sky. Amazing, shining runes shimmered just beneath the current.

Merlin's ears swiveled. He padded along the bank, tail swishing from side to side.

From the water rose a slow, deliberate shape. A large turtle with a shell domed like a boulder, with the color of warm earth and eyes as deep as mountain wells.

"I am Tiko," he rumbled. "Guardian of Crossings. No one shall pass without respect for the river's ancient history and sacred memory."

Lila knelt. "What must we do to cross?"

"Just listen," Tiko said simply.

The river gurgled, carrying fragments of voices. Laughter of children long grown, songs sung by families picnicking by its banks.

Lila sketched the rippling sounds, her pencil strokes catching music on paper.

Merlin bowed his head, acknowledging the river's living history.

Satisfied, Tiko lowered his broad shell. "Climb on and I shall carry you across."

FUN FACT:

Rivers carry not just water, but also history.
They shape the land, provide homes for
animals and
people and store memories through the life
they support.

Chapter 5
Turtle Bridge

They crossed safely, but the path ended at a series of stones stretching across a rushing stream. Each stone bore a carved face and each face wore a different expression.

"The Bridge with a Smile," Oliver explained from a branch overhead. "It will only let you cross if you can match it's joy."

Lila bit her lip. The first stone frowned. Merlin leapt lightly onto it, his tail flicking. Instantly the stone's frown softened into a grin.

Lila laughed and followed, balancing carefully. Each time Merlin stepped, the stones brightened, their faces curving into smiles. By the time they reached the last stone, the whole bridge was glowing with delight.

"You see?" said Oliver. "Sometimes courage is as simple as carrying with you and sharing your joy"

FUN FACT:

Smiling and sharing joy can make challenges easier. Positive emotions can change how people, and even situations, respond to us.

Chapter 6
Lantern Beetles

Night began to fall, shadows stretching long. From the grass rose a soft pulsing light. Then another. Then dozens. Dozens and dozens of fireflies.

"Lantern beetles", whispered Lila. Their shells glowed green and gold, painting the dusk like starlight.

Merlin crouched low, eyes huge, as the magical bugs drifted and illuminated around him like amazing, magical sparks.

Lila reached out and one landed on her finger like a soft glowing whisper, it's light warm, but gentle.

"They light the way to truth," Oliver said softly. "Follow their illuminated trail."

The mystical fireflies hovered into the forest. Lila and Merlin followed, their path glowing with wonder.

FUN FACT:

Some beetles and insects' glow in the dark because of bioluminescence, a natural chemical reaction in their bodies that creates an illuminating glow.

Chapter 7
Puzzles in the Half-Light

Deep in the forest, the fireflies gathered around a cluster of rocks etched with glowing symbols. The light was dim, exposing neither day nor night. Half-light.

Merlin padded forward, pawing at the symbols. As he touched one, it lit up. Lila knelt and copied the shapes into her sketchbook, trying to understand.

"It's a puzzle," she murmured. She traced the lines until they formed a picture. A tree with roots entwined around a star.

"Knowledge is found not in rushing," Oliver said, "but in patience."

With Merlin's careful paws and Lila's sketches, the runes aligned, and the rocks split and divided apart, revealing a narrow path, welcoming the ambitious pair to continue on their adventurous journey.

FUN FACT:

Solving puzzles teaches patience. Many puzzles are based on patterns, and paying close attention, applying deep thought and allowing much patience can unlock the hidden answers.

Chapter 8
Whispering Stones

The path led to a clearing filled with mossy stones, each taller than Lila. They hummed faintly, whispers threading the air.

Merlin tilted his head, listening. His ears twitched as though the stones spoke directly to him. Lila pressed her ear to one and gasped. She heard voices of guardians past, protectors of the land, keepers of the secrets.

"They remember all who walked before," Oliver explained. "They test whether you carry respect for their history." Lila drew the stones faithfully in her sketchbook, honoring them. Merlin bowed his head. The whispers swelled into harmony, granting passage deeper into the forest.

FUN FACT:

Rocks and stones hold history. Fossils and layers of rock can tell us about Earth's past, just like the Whispering Stones remember children and guardians.

Chapter 9
The Hidden Grove

At last, the fireflies rose in swirls, guiding them to a secret hidden grove.

Trees arched in a circle, their leaves shimmering with silver veins like the first leaf that wandered through the air, down the paths, across the river and to the garden, to be discovered by it's welcomed guests. A secret invitation.

The ground glowed faintly. In the center of the grove, Merlin and Lila stood side by side, bathed in the soft green-gold light of fireflies, as they performed their illuminated presence.

Lila caught her breath. "It's beautiful!"

Merlin's tail curled around her ankle. His eyes reflected the firefly light, as if he had always belonged here.

"This is the Hidden Grove," Oliver said. "Few find it. Very few are granted a welcome. Those invited are extremely rare and few."

FUN FACT:

Forests and groves are home to countless plants and animals. Protecting even small patches of nature helps keep our entire environment healthy and stable.

Chapter 10
The Last Test

In the heart of the grove stood a tiny sapling, weak and leaning. It's leaves glowed only faintly and drooped sadly. Without help, it would not survive.

"This is your final test," Oliver said. "Will you nurture what cannot reward you?"

Lila knelt, propping the sapling upright with her kind,

gentle hands. Merlin stood beside her, tail fluffed, green eyes watchful. Together, they supported the fragile life.

The sapling brightened, straightening with strength. New leaves unfurled, silver veins glowing with gratitude. Returned was it's life that was nearly lost, it's hope restored.

"You have passed," Oliver said warmly. "For true guardians protect not for glory or pride, but with a caring heart full of love for life"

FUN FACT:

Young trees, called saplings, need support as they grow. With care, they grow strong roots and branches, just like kids grow strong with love and support.

Chapter 11
The Promise

Night deepened. Lanterns hung from unseen branches, lighting the grove in golden glow. Fireflies joined their light until the whole clearing shimmered.

Lila hugged her sketchbook to her chest. Merlin sat beside her, eyes half-closed in contentment.

"I promise to always listen and to care," Lila whispered.

Merlin gave a soft purr, his promise unspoken but clear.

Together, under lanterns and fireflies, they sealed a bond stronger than words. A promise of care and love never to be broken.

FUN FACT:

Promises are very powerful.
Keeping them builds trust, loyalty,
friendships, sincerity and bonds,
just like lanterns lighting the dark
remind us of warmth, safety,
security, comfort and hope.

Chapter 12
Edges and Middles

Morning returned them to the garden. The silver leaf fluttered once more and dissolved forever into light.

Merlin perched proudly on the fence, his plume tail curling.

Lila sat cross-legged in the grass, sketchbook open, drawing him in the rising morning sun.

Their great adventure was over, yet something remained.

A new knowledge.

A knowledge of knowing that edges and endings were really just new beginnings.

Merlin blinked slowly at Lila, and she smiled back.

In their hearts, they carried the grove, the owl, the turtle, the whispers and the promise.

And every morning after, when Merlin claimed his windowsill and Lila opened her sketchbook, they secretly knew of the magic that was never far.

FUN FACT:

Every ending can also be a new beginning. Stories, just like life, are made of both edges and middles, beginnings and endings, with each chapter leading to the next beginning, the next adventure.

The End

About the Author

Sandi Sanders has always believed that animals carry secrets just beyond human senses. Inspired by real-life Somali cats and exploring their playful antics, she imagines stories that invite young dreamers, seekers and explorers to discover wonder and adventure in the everyday.

9 781806 237623